DISNEY
PRINCESS
MOVIE THEATER
STORYBOOK

Adapted by Rita Balducci

Contents

 Reader's Digest Children's Books™

Pleasantville, New York • Montréal, Québec • Bath, UK

Cinderella

DISK I

1 Once upon a time, there was a lovely young girl who lived with her widowed father. She was happy and kind to all. However, her father felt that she needed a mother, and in time he married **2** a woman with two young daughters of her own.

When her dear father died, the young girl soon learned the true natures of her cruel Stepmother and stepsisters. They called her **3** Cinderella and forced her to do all the work of the household. She sang as she cooked and cleaned and never complained about her hard life. Cinderella dreamed that someday the wishes dear to her heart would come true, and she would find true

love and happiness. The barnyard animals became her companions, and she was so gentle that even the birds and mice did not fear her. Gus and Jaq were two mice that Cinderella fed and

4 dressed. They loved her dearly and wished they could do something to help her.

One day, an invitation arrived from the royal palace. "There's to be a ball," the Stepmother read. "Every eligible maiden is to attend."

"Why, I can go, too!" Cinderella cried.

[5] Her Stepmother agreed, *if* Cinderella managed to finish her work. Gus and Jaq and the other mice and birds decided to surprise

[6] Cinderella. They sewed a lovely gown while she worked at her chores.

Cinderella was overjoyed to find the beautiful dress in her attic room. She put it on and rushed to join her stepsisters.

7 "Look! That's my sash!" cried one in a jealous rage.

"Those are my beads!" shrieked the other. They tore at Cinderella's dress until it was tattered and

8 ruined. Poor Cinderella ran to the garden in despair.

As she wept, Cinderella became aware of a gentle hand stroking her hair and a soft voice speaking to her.

"Who are you?" Cinderella asked the kindly woman.

"Why, I'm your Fairy Godmother, child," the woman said. "I've come to help you get to the ball." Then, with a wave of her wand, the mice changed into horses and a pumpkin became a glittering coach.

DISK 2

9

Cinderella was speechless. With another wave of her wand, the Fairy Godmother changed Cinderella's raggedy dress to a beautiful, shimmering gown. Cinderella looked down—she was even wearing sparkling glass slippers!

10

"You must leave the ball before midnight," the Fairy Godmother told her, "for then the spell will be broken."

As soon as Cinderella entered the ballroom, the Prince could not take his eyes off her. They danced under the light of the moon, and before long, they had fallen in love.

Suddenly, a chime sounded from high above. The clock had begun to strike the midnight hour. "I must go!" Cinderella cried as she ran from the ballroom. In her hurry, one glass shoe slipped from her foot.

The Prince picked up the delicate slipper. "I will marry the maiden whose foot fits this slipper," he declared.

11

12

The Grand Duke and his footman set out at dawn to find the owner of the glass slipper. In time, they came to **13** Cinderella's house and were relieved to see that the slipper fit neither of the unpleasant stepsisters.

What the Grand Duke did not know was that Cinderella had been locked away in the attic by her evil Stepmother. Gus and **14** Jaq bravely stole the key and slid it under the door to free Cinderella just in time.

Just as the Grand Duke and his footman were preparing to leave with the slipper, Cinderella called to him. "Your Grace! Please wait. May I try it on?"

The wicked Stepmother sneered, but there was nothing she could do. Or was there? Just as the footman passed her, she tripped him with her cane. The glass slipper flew from his hands and shattered at Cinderella's feet.

The Grand Duke gasped in dismay. Just then, Cinderella spoke, "But you see, I have the other slipper." She held out the matching shoe to the delight of the Grand Duke and the horror of her stepmother. It fit her foot perfectly!

Cinderella's dreams had come true! The Prince and Cinderella were married right away, and they lived happily ever after.

Beauty and the Beast

*I*n a small town in France, a long time ago, there lived a girl named Belle. She was smart and kind, and she dreamed of leaving her small town to have adventures like the ones she read about in books. Gaston, a vain hunter, hoped to make Belle his wife, but she was not the least bit interested in marrying him.

Belle was quite devoted to her father, an absent-minded inventor. He understood Belle's dreams and wishes, and he loved her more than anything else in the world.

One evening, Belle's father became lost in the woods. He came upon an enormous castle and entered it. To his surprise, he found that the furniture inside was

DISK I

1

2

3

enchanted. He was even more astonished when a candlestick named Lumiere and a clock named Cogsworth greeted him and welcomed him to the castle.

Suddenly, he heard a fierce growl, and an enormous beast appeared and cornered him. "Please, I mean no harm!" Belle's father begged, but the Beast took him prisoner.

4

When her father didn't come home, Belle set out to search the forest where he had gone. In time, she, too came to the Beast's enchanted castle. She found her father locked in a dungeon in the castle.

5

"You must go right now!" her father warned. But Belle would not leave and she begged the Beast to let her take her father's place as prisoner. The Beast agreed. There was a spell over the castle, and the Beast knew that if Belle came to love him, the spell would be broken. Then he and the enchanted furniture would return to their original human forms.

6 Belle missed her father terribly, but she also found the castle to be a strange and wonderful place. The Beast told her she was free to wander throughout the castle, except for one room which she was forbidden to enter. One day, Belle's curiosity got the better of her and she decided to sneak into the forbidden room. Inside, she found a

7 rose under a bell jar, glittering and magical.

Just then the Beast bounded into the room. He was furious that Belle had disobeyed him. "What are you doing here?" he shouted angrily. Belle was terrified. She had never seen the Beast this angry.

Belle fled the castle and ran into the forest. A pack of hungry wolves chased her through the snow. As they were about to attack, the Beast appeared and chased them off, saving Belle's life.

DISK 2

Belle began to look at the Beast differently after he saved her. Soon they became good friends. Lumiere, Cogsworth, and the rest of their castle friends were very excited to see the change in the Beast. It seemed as though the spell was finally going to be broken!

One evening, the Beast decided to tell Belle that he loved her. They shared a romantic evening of dancing under the stars. "Are you happy, Belle?" he gently asked her. Belle told the Beast that she

would be happy if she could just see her father again.

With a heavy heart, the Beast said, "You are no longer my prisoner. Take this magical mirror to remember me."

11 Belle's father was overjoyed to see his daughter again. She told him how the Beast had changed, and of the many kind things he had done for her. A knock at the door interrupted them.

It was Gaston and a crowd of villagers. Belle's father had been telling tales about a strange beast, but no one had believed him. They all thought he was crazy and had come to take him to the insane asylum!

"I can help you and your father, Belle," Gaston said. "*If* you agree to marry me."

"Never!" cried Belle.

12 Gaston picked up the magical mirror and he saw a reflection of the Beast. "So this is who you care for?" he sneered. He turned to the villagers and shouted,

"We must kill this wicked beast!" The angry villagers followed Gaston into the forest, determined to kill the Beast.

Gaston soon found the Beast in the **13** forbidden tower room. They fought on the slippery castle rooftop. Gaston drew a knife and stabbed the Beast. Suddenly, **14** Gaston lost his footing and fell.

"Beast!" Belle cried, rushing to where he lay wounded. Tears fell from her eyes as she leaned forward, whispering "I love you."

Slowly, the Beast rose into the air and began to change. Belle watched in astonishment as brilliant beams of light began to dance around him. As his cloak twisted and spun, the Beast was transformed into a handsome young man.

15

"Belle," he said, holding his hand out to her. Belle looked deeply into the young man's blue eyes. She suddenly realized that the handsome young man and the Beast were one and the same. "It's you!" she cried happily.

As the Beast was transformed, so were the rest of the people from his castle. Soon afterward, they all celebrated the wedding of Beauty and the Beast, and everyone lived happily ever after.

16

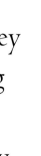

The Little Mermaid

Deep under the sea, a royal concert was about to begin. King Triton had invited all the merpeople to hear his youngest daughter, Ariel, sing with her sisters. Sebastian the crab had great confidence in Ariel's debut, and his chest swelled with pride as a

DISK 1

clamshell popped open to reveal...nothing. Ariel had forgotten about the concert!

Instead, she was busy exploring the wreck of a sunken ship with her fish friend Flounder. They

suddenly got a big surprise.

"Shark!" Flounder shouted in a panic. Ariel and Flounder escaped just in time.

3 But they weren't entirely out of danger. The evil sea witch Ursula had been watching them from a magic bubble. Ursula hated King Triton and began to plot against him. "King Triton's daughter may be very useful to me," Ursula decided.

King Triton was furious about Ariel missing the concert. When he found out she had been up to the surface of the sea, he knew something had to be done. The king believed that the surface was a dangerous place. He put Sebastian in charge of keeping Ariel out of trouble.

4 Ariel swam to her hidden cave. "I wish I could know what it would be like to live on land," she sighed. She had treasures that she had collected from sunken ships, but they only gave her a glimpse of what humans were really like.

Ariel looked up to see the shadow of a ship overhead. "Ariel, wait!" cried Sebastian, but it was too late.

Ariel watched as sailors sang and danced on the ship's deck. She couldn't help noticing a handsome young man among them.

"Happy birthday, Prince Eric," said an older man as he unveiled a statue of the dashing prince.

5 Suddenly, a storm blew in. Lightning flashed and the wind howled. Ariel watched as the ship tossed in the waves. Prince Eric was thrown overboard!

Ariel dove under the water and pulled the unconscious prince to shore. She had never been so close to a human before. She sang to him softly until he began to wake up. Just then, a dog's barking startled her, and she quickly slipped back into the sea.

"There was a girl," the prince told his friend, Sir Grimsby. "She had the most beautiful voice. She saved me." He had fallen in love with the mysterious young woman.

Ariel had fallen in love, too. King Triton noticed how

happy she was, but when he learned that she had disobeyed him and saved a human, he lost his temper. With one wave of his arm, King Triton destroyed all of Ariel's treasures.

7

Ariel was quite upset with her father. *He doesn't understand me or that I must follow my own heart. And my heart leads me to Prince Eric. I must see the prince again,* Ariel thought, *even if I have to go to Ursula to do it!*

Ursula told Ariel that she

could become a human for three days. At the end of that time, the prince would have to give her a kiss of true love if she were to remain with him always.

"And if he doesn't, you turn back into a mermaid, and you belong to me!" Ursula cackled. "Oh, yes, we must talk about the price. You must give me...your voice!"

Ariel knew that Ursula could not be trusted, but she longed to be with Prince Eric once more. She signed the agreement. Immediately, she began to change. Her tail turned into legs, and she could no longer breathe underwater. She swam to the surface, gasping for air. When Ariel reached the shallow waters offshore, she gazed in wonder at her new legs.

Ariel discovered that life on land was even more exciting than she had ever dreamed. *So this is what it is like to have legs!* Ariel thought.

Prince Eric was instantly enchanted with Ariel. He invited her to stay at the palace and took her for a **10** tour of the kingdom. Ariel desperately wished there was some way to let him know who she really was. Time was running out!

Flounder, Sebastian, and Scuttle the seagull tried to help the romance along. Sebastian crooned a love song as Prince **11** Eric leaned over to kiss Ariel. Suddenly, their boat tipped over! Flotsam and Jetsam, Ursula's pet eels, had ruined the lovely moment.

"That was too close," Ursula decided. She came ashore disguised as **12** a beautiful woman to distract Eric. Using Ariel's voice and her own hypnotic power, she tricked the prince into thinking that she was the one who had rescued him.

"We will be married today," Eric said, falling under her spell. He took the hand of his bride-to-be. Ariel was heartbroken. She sat on the dock and watched as the wedding ship sailed off into the sunset.

Scuttle flew over the ship and recognized Ursula on board. When Ariel **13** learned the true identity of the woman Eric planned to marry, she knew she had to stop the wedding.

As the ceremony began, flocks of seagulls attacked the wedding party. The shell which held Ariel's voice was torn from Ursula's necklace. Ariel's voice escaped and returned to Ariel.

"Eric!" Ariel cried. Ursula's spell was broken. The prince realized that Ariel was the woman who had saved him. He leaned forward to kiss her.

"You're too late!" shrieked Ursula as huge, black tentacles burst forth from her body. Ursula grabbed Ariel, who had turned back into a mermaid, and pulled her under the water.

King Triton tried to stop Ursula from taking his daughter. "Take me instead," he said. Ursula agreed. With the king's trident in hand, she became huge.

14

15

Then suddenly Prince Eric steered the bow of the ship right into Ursula, putting an end to her forever.

When King Triton saw how deeply Ariel and Eric loved each other, he knew he had no choice but to grant them their wish to be married. He changed Ariel back into a human, and with humans and merpeople looking on, Ariel and Eric were married at sea. At last, Ariel's dreams had come true!

16

Sleeping Beauty

Once upon a time, there was a king named Stefan. When King Stefan's daughter, Aurora, was born, he invited everyone in the kingdom to join him in a great feast to celebrate the happy occasion. King Hubert and his young son, Phillip, were among the guests, for it had already been decided that Phillip and Aurora would marry someday.

Three good fairies named Flora, Fauna, and Merryweather were also invited, and they came with gifts for the child. Flora gave the baby the gift of beauty.

DISK I

1

Fauna gave the child the gift of song. But before Merryweather could give her gift,

the evil fairy Maleficent appeared. She was angry she had not been invited, so she put a curse on the baby. "Before the sun sets on her sixteenth birthday," Maleficent declared, "she will prick her finger on the spindle of a spinning wheel...and die!"

2 Maleficent's power was so strong that neither Flora, Fauna, nor Merryweather could completely undo the curse. But because Merryweather had not yet given her gift, she was able to change the curse. Instead of dying, the princess would fall asleep and remain that way until she received a kiss from her true love.

To protect Aurora, the fairies took her to a cottage in the woods where they lovingly raised her. So no one would know who she was, the fairies changed her name to Briar Rose.

[3] [4] Briar Rose grew up not knowing she was a princess, but she was beautiful and good. On her sixteenth birthday, the fairies sent her out to pick berries so they could make her a special dress. Briar Rose happily obeyed her dear friends.

5 As Briar Rose walked through the woods, she began to sing a love song. Her voice was so beautiful that all the woodland animals gathered to listen.

6 A young man on horseback heard the singing, too, and he rode toward the sweet-sounding voice. He was enchanted by Briar Rose's song and he began to sing along with her. At first, she was startled to see the young man and hear his strong voice joining with her own. He seemed like a prince out of one of her dreams. She was captivated by the young man.

7 They danced together as they sang, and by the end of the duet, the two young people had fallen deeply in love.

When Briar Rose arrived back at the
cottage, she breathlessly told the fairies
that she had fallen in love with a young
man in the woods. It was then that the
fairies had to tell her the truth about her
birth and her name. She was heartbroken
to learn that she was truly a princess, and
was already betrothed to Prince Phillip.
With a heavy heart, Aurora walked with
the fairies back to her father's castle.

Aurora was home at last, but her mind
was on her true love. Suddenly, a strange
green light caught her eye. She followed
the light all the way to the tallest tower in

8

DISK 2

9

the castle, where a spinning wheel glowed in the corner. The fairies realized Aurora was in danger, and they raced to stop her from touching the spinning wheel. But before they could stop her, Aurora pricked her finger on the spindle. She instantly fell to the floor and lay motionless.

The fairies laid Aurora gently on her bed. "The king and queen will be heartbroken," they said. "To save them from this

10 heartache, we must put everyone else in the kingdom to sleep."

At the very same time, the young man with whom Aurora had fallen in love came to the cottage looking for her. Instead **11** he met the evil Maleficent. Maleficent knew the young man was really Prince Phillip, and she quickly chained him in her dungeon.

The good fairies soon discovered his **12** true identity and came to his rescue. They freed the prince and gave him a magic sword and shield to fight Maleficent. Prince Phillip slashed his way through the **13** brambles surrounding the castle. Maleficent turned herself into a huge dragon and set fire to the brambles.

Prince Phillip bravely fought the

14 dragon, using his sword to kill the evil creature. Then he raced to Aurora's side and kissed her. The spell was broken! Aurora's eyes

15 opened to see the face of the young man she loved, and all over the kingdom, everyone else awoke, too. The

16 fairies were overjoyed as the happy pair joined hands. True love had conquered all!

Snow White

DISK I

1 Once upon a time, in a faraway land, there lived a young princess named Snow White. She was as beautiful as she was good. Even the little birds trusted and loved her. It wasn't long before a handsome prince also fell in love with Snow White, and she with him.

Snow White lived in the castle of the cruel and jealous Queen. The Queen began each day by asking her Magic Mirror to tell her the name of the fairest maiden in all the land. On the day the Mirror replied, "Snow White," the Queen decided that the beautiful young princess must die.

The Queen summoned her Huntsman and ordered him to take the young girl's life. The Huntsman, however, was a good man, and he couldn't bring himself to kill the beautiful princess. He fell to his knees and revealed the wicked plot to Snow White. Terrified, Snow White ran deep into the woods. It seemed that hundreds of eyes were watching her, and she fell, sobbing, to the ground.

Snow White soon realized that the watchful eyes belonged to the gentle woodland creatures who only wanted to help her. They led her to a tiny cottage in the woods. It was the home of the Seven Dwarfs who were at work in the diamond mines. Grateful to be safe at last, Snow White lay down on the tiny beds and fell fast asleep.

6

Snow White woke up to find herself surrounded by the Dwarfs. She told them what had happened. They were anxious to protect the young princess, so they invited her to stay with them. Snow White promised to cook and clean for them, and even bake gooseberry pies. All the Dwarfs— except for Grumpy, who didn't trust anyone— shouted, "Hurray! She stays!"

7

Snow White began tidying up the
cottage and making a delicious meal for
her new friends. The Dwarfs wanted to
make Snow White
happy, so they even
washed up
before supper
just to please
her. After
the meal,

they sang and
danced long
into the night.

When the Queen learned from her Magic Mirror that Snow White was still

DISK 2
[9]

alive, she devised an evil plan to get rid of her once and for all. First, she drank a potion that turned her into an old peddler woman. Then she made a poison apple to

[10]

give to the innocent girl.

[11]

The next morning, as the Dwarfs left for the mines, Snow White gave each of them a kiss goodbye on the forehead.

Once the Dwarfs were gone, the

[12]

Queen approached the Dwarfs' house, carrying a basket of apples on her arm.

Snow White took pity on the
wretched-looking woman at her door and
invited her inside.

"Thank you for your kindness," said
the old woman. "To repay you, here is a
wishing apple. Just one bite, and all your
dreams will come true."

Snow White took the apple
and wished for the Prince
to come and take her
away. But after one bite,
Snow White fell down
as if she were dead.

13

When the forest animals learned what had happened, they raced to find the Seven Dwarfs. "We must help the princess!" the Dwarfs cried. They dropped their axes and ran towards their house. Along the way, they encountered the Queen. They chased her to the edge of a steep cliff, where she slipped and fell to her death.

When the Dwarfs returned home and saw the still, silent figure of Snow White, they were heartbroken. They could not bear the thought of burying her, so they kept watch over her day and night.

14

One day, the Prince happened to pass by the Dwarfs' house. When he saw Snow White, he recognized his true love at once. He bent to kiss her. Suddenly, Snow White's eyes fluttered open. The kiss had broken the Queen's spell! The Prince lifted Snow White onto his horse and they bid farewell to the loyal Dwarfs. Snow White and the Prince lived happily ever after.

15

16